# Curious George®

## Plays Mini Golf

**Adaptation by Marcy Goldberg Sacks**
**Based on the TV series teleplay**
**written by Craig Miller**

Houghton Mifflin Company
Boston 2008

For information about permission to reproduce selections from this book, write to
Permissions, Houghton Mifflin Company, 215 Park Avenue South, New York, New York 10003.

Library of Congress Cataloging-in-Publication Data is on file.

Design by Afsoon Razavi and Marcy Goldberg Sacks

www.houghtonmifflinbooks.com

Printed in Singapore
TWP 10 9 8 7 6 5 4 3 2 1

George and Steve were good friends.
They liked to play games.
Steve always had the high score.
He always won.

One day Steve invited George to
play mini golf.
This was a new game for George.
He was curious.
Maybe he could win this time.

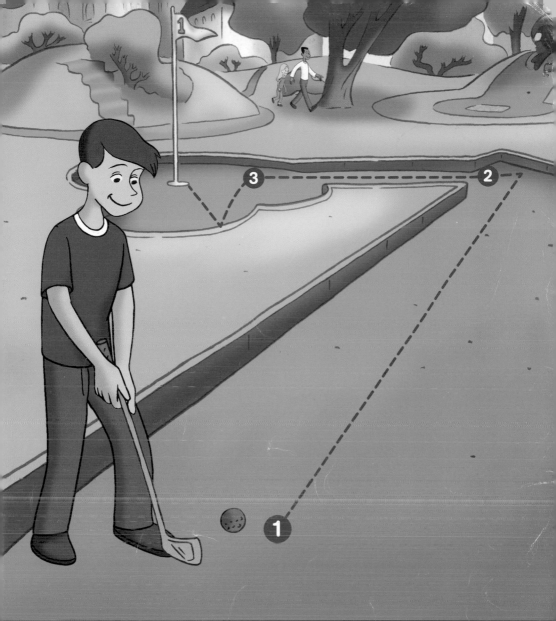

Steve hit the ball one . . . two . . .
three times.
Now it was George's turn.

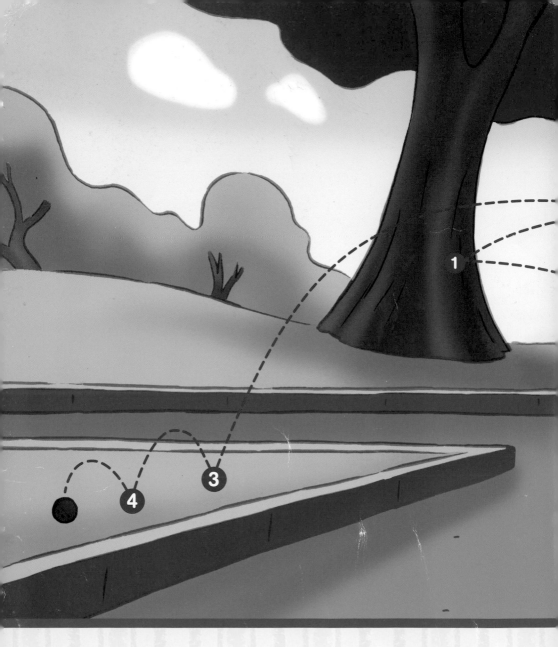

George took a big swing.
His ball hit two trees!

George swung his golf club
many times to get a high score.

George hit the ball again and
again and again.

It went all over the golf course.
Golf was easy!

George hit the ball as many times as he could.
Finally, he hit it right into the hole.

At the end of the game, Steve read
the scores:
Steve, 35, Betsy, 58, and George . . .
250!

George had the highest score.
He was so happy.
He had won.

"But George, in golf the *lowest*
score is best," Betsy told him.
"I won the game," Steve said.

George was surprised.
How could a small number be
better than a big number?

George had an idea.
He wanted to win in golf.
He had to practice.
George asked his friend if he
could borrow some things from
their house.

George made a golf course on the roof!
A paper towel roll was his club.
He blew in one end.
Air came out the other end.

The ball moved.
He was ready to play.
George invited Steve over.

George played first.
He blew through the tube . . . and got
a hole in one!

Steve was next.
But it took him eight tries to get
the ball into the hole.

Steve counted the points.
George had the lowest score.
Finally he was the winner — of
monkey mini golf!

# Understanding Numbers

**3** **5** **1** **4** **2**

Numbers can mean different things depending on where they are used. For example, a larger number isn't always best (as in a golf score). In other cases, such as addresses, numbers hold no value other than as markers or identifiers.

## Birthday Countdown

Fill in the calendar of the month of your birthday. Circle your birthday. Then, starting with the first of the month mark a big X through each day and count down (though it's actually forward!) until you reach the big day.

### Your Birthday Month

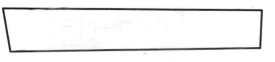

| S | M | T | W | T | F | S |
|---|---|---|---|---|---|---|
|   |   |   |   |   |   |   |
|   |   |   |   |   |   |   |
|   |   |   |   |   |   |   |
|   |   |   |   |   |   |   |

## Counting Up, Counting Down

The next time you walk down the street, look at the numbers on the buildings. Are they getting bigger or smaller? What if you turned around and walked in the other direction? Is one building better than another just because its number is bigger?

# Mini Mini Golf

George used "found objects" to make his own mini golf course. You can do the same using household items like these:

ruler and dry sponge, rubber ball or marbles, paper, tape, scissors, cardboard boxes, paper towel rolls, cotton towels, paper plates, a coffee can, building blocks, or other toys

## Instructions:

1. Make a golf club by taping a sponge to the bottom of a ruler.
2. Draw pictures of your ideas for a golf course. Choose one you can build with materials you have.
3. Build your course (see ideas below) using the coffee can as the final hole.
4. Take turns with a friend playing your way through.
5. Talk about what's working and what's not. Do you need to change your design?

## Ideas for your golf course:

- Make a tunnel by taping a paper towel roll on the floor.
- Put a chair or stool in the room for your ball to go under.
- Place paper plates on the floor to create obstacles for your ball to go around.
- Make a "sand trap" from a towel.
- Use two rows of building blocks to create a straight pathway.
- Come up with your own creative ideas!